Praise for Matt Haig and Chris Mould

'Absolutely brilliant'
CBBC

'Uplifting . . . Short and very sweet'
Guardian

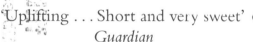

'Amazing'
Blue Peter

'The perfect package of happiness'
Olivia Colman

ACC. No: 07050949

Also by Matt Haig

THE TRUTH PIXIE

GOES TO SCHOOL

MATT HAIG

with illustrations by

CHRIS MOULD

CANONGATE

First published in Great Britain, the USA and Canada in 2019
by Canongate Books Ltd,
14 High Street, Edinburgh EH1 1TE

Distributed in the USA by Publishers Group West
and in Canada by Publishers Group Canada

canongate.co.uk

1

Copyright © Matt Haig, 2019
Illustrations copyright © Chris Mould, 2019

The moral rights of the author and the illustrator have been asserted

British Library Cataloguing-in-Publication Data
A catalogue record for this book is available on
request from the British Library

ISBN 978 1 78689 826 5

Typeset by Biblichor Ltd, Edinburgh

Printed and bound in Great Britain
by Clays Ltd, Elcograf S.p.A.

To Pearl and Lucas

There once was a girl
Who lived far away,
And who tried to be kind,
Whatever the day.

This girl was called **Aada**.

She lived with her dad.

She was sometimes happy,

But now she was sad.

She'd had a bad year,
She'd had to move town,
And start a new school,
And wear a new frown.

Her gran had died,
Her dad lost his job.
Aada spent the whole year
Trying not to sob.

But this isn't a sad story –

Not really, no –

Because Aada
had
a
Pixie,
Wherever
she would go.

The pixie lived
In Aada's house,
And in her hair
Was Marta the mouse.

This pixie slept
Under Aada's bed,
And Aada trusted
Whatever she said.

5

You see . . .

Wherever she was,
Whatever the day,
The Truth Pixie had
Just one thing to say.

Just as cats go miaow and cows go MOO The PiXiE could ONLY say things that were true.

And Aada was pleased

That she had such a friend.

She hoped that these days

Would never end.

When the Truth Pixie and Aada
Went into town,
They'd laugh when they saw
Everyone frown.

'Hello,' said Aada.
'We'd like a loaf of bread.'
'No pixies allowed!'
The shopkeeper said.

'Well!' said the pixie.
'That's just rude!
Especially when you sell
Such disgusting food!'

Back at home
With Aada and her dad,
She watched the news
But it drove her mad.

'Why do humans chop down trees
When forests are so fantastic?
And why do you clog your oceans
With all that horrible plastic?'

Aada's dad sighed.
'It's not that simple.'
Aada agreed with the pixie
As she picked at a pimple.

Aada loved the pixie.
They had great times together,
Such as snowball fights
In wintry weather.

13

Aada told her stories,
Made up in her head,
And the pixie listened closely
To everything she said.

Aada played piano,
The pixie sang along,
And they both laughed happily
Whenever it went wrong.

When Aada was happy,
The pixie was there.
(The best kind of happy
Is the kind you can share.)

And when times were tough,
And when Aada felt bad,
The pixie was there
To make her less sad.

She told Aada the truth,
She told her what was real,
She told her it's okay
To feel what she feels.

Aada started a new school,
And the pixie came too.

But this school was a place
Where it was hard to be true.

'Infinity,' said the maths teacher,
'Is the largest number ever!'
'Nope,' said the pixie.
'Oh,' Teacher sighed. 'So you think you are clever?'

'Not really,' said the pixie.
'But there's a rabbit called Bangly-Bon,
Who says there's a number that's

infinity
Plus
One

In a history lesson,
The pixie was amused,
Because history was a subject
That left her confused.

'It seems strange,'
She told the very strict teacher,
'That your history
Is full of only one creature.'

'There are no dogs,
Pixies or even elves.
It seems like humans
Are obsessed with themselves!'

Aada was embarrassed,
     And turned bright red,
          Every time the pixie
               Said what she said.

And outside, later on,
When the lesson was sports,
The pixie was laughed at,
In her silly yellow shorts.

She couldn't catch a ball
And she couldn't run fast,
And in every single race
She always came last.

23

The children thought
The pixie was strange.
They laughed at her difference
And they **didn't** like change.

The Truth Pixie didn't mind,

She really didn't care.

(And nor did the mouse

Who lived in her hair.)

The trouble was
That Aada **did** care,
Because the children at school
Would always be there.

There was one girl
Whose name was Leena.
She had cold eyes
And couldn't be **meaner**.

She laughed at Aada
And her pixie friend,
So Aada tried to be normal,
But couldn't pretend.

'You aren't **normal**' –
That's what Leena told her.
Aada closed her eyes,
And wished she was older.

'You never smile
And you talk really funny.
Your clothes are shabby
And you've got no money.

You hang out with a pixie,
And cry when you're sad,
You live in a tiny house
With your weird old dad.

And this Pixie of yours,
Why is she with you?
She's soooo very rude,
And she smells of PoO.

Pixies are evil,
Pixies are bad,
If you live with a Pixie,
You end up mad.'

Aada was quiet,
Aada couldn't speak.
Aada's legs
Felt really weak.

The pixie was there,
And she got really cross.

She had to show this girl
Who was actually the **boss**.

'You ask me why
I smell of poo.
It's 'cos the mouse in my hair
Has got no loo.

And listen, why must you always
Pick on Aada?
Why must you try
To make her life harder?

Pixies aren't evil,
Pixies aren't bad.
I hate your lies,
'Cos they make me sad.'

Leena leaned in,

'You're really
so strange,
Why can't you
be normal?

Why can't
you change?'

'Well, you see,
You can't fix me,
Because I'm an actual

. . . **Truth Pixie.**

I tell the truth
In what I say.
I tell it at night
And I tell it all day.

And the truth about you,
I can explain fully:
You're being a nasty,
Insecure bully.

You pick on others
To make you feel better,
Which is like trying to dry
By getting even wetter.

I'll give you some advice,
I hope you don't mind.

But you won't
feel good
Until you are
kind

35

I know you get scared
Of a million things -
Spiders and shadows
And bats with
their wings.

You don't like to hear
A dog loudly bark,
And you lie in bed,
Afraid of the dark.

Leena stared at the pixie
And stamped her feet.
'You are such a **freak**!
And you **think** you're sweet.

You're not a human,
You shouldn't be here,
With your silly voice
And your pointy ears.

I think it's funny that Aada
Has no friends,
Except a pixie
Whose truth never ends.'

She grabbed the pixie,
Dangled her above the ground,
As Maarta the mouse
Squeaked a frightened sound.

'Please,' said Aada,
'Leave her alone.'
But into the air
The pixie was thrown.

She flew down the corridor
Where Aada couldn't reach her
And landed in the arms
Of their least favourite teacher.

'Pixie!' said the teacher.
'What are you doing?'
'Ummm, I was flung in the air
By Leena Gruing.'

And from that day on,
Things got even worse.
The Truth Pixie felt less like a friend
And more like a **curse**.

One day, Aada,
Wishing no one could see her,
Saw there in her path
That bully Leena.

'Please,' Aada said,
'I've got to go to class.'
But Leena stood in the way
And wouldn't let her past.

Aada pushed her and ran
And didn't look back.
It felt like the whole school
Was on the attack.

People laughed in class,
Ignored her at break.
There wasn't a single
Friend it seemed she could make.

The Truth Pixie sighed
When she saw this sad stuff,
And wished she could tell Aada
She was more than enough.

'Oh, Aada, I'm sorry
About these people at school.
I had no idea
Humans could be so cruel.'

'But it's the truth,' said Aada.
'I really am a bit strange.
I wish I was normal,
I wish I could change.

I wish I could speak
Like the others do.
I wish I could smile
And not look so blue.

I wish I didn't care about people
Who make me a **joke**.
I wish we had **money**
And weren't so **broke**.

I wish I had their faces
With their natural smiles.
And I wish I didn't have thoughts
Like snapping crocodiles.

I wish Mum was still here,
And my gran too.
But I know, at least,
That **I still have you**.'

'Oh, thank you,' said the pixie.
'That's good to hear.
But I don't like to see
Your mind full of fear.

You're not normal,
That much is true.
But why be normal,
When you could also be you?

Don't try to be something
You really are not.
Your one true self
Is the best thing
you've got.

49

If everyone was normal,
All of the time,
Life would be a poem
With only one rhyme.

The best people I've met
Were always rather weird,
Like that man Father Christmas,
With his funny clothes and beard.

And the Easter Bunny,
With long ears and silly short legs,
Who gives the world chocolate
That is turned into EGGS!!!'

Aada smiled,
But still looked sad.
The Truth Pixie felt
Really quite bad.

Late at night,
There was no denying,
The sound from the bed
Was the sound of crying.

'I'm sorry,' said the pixie.
'This is all my fault,'
As Aada shed a tear
That tasted of salt.

At school the next day,
The pixie kept out of sight,
So Aada could make friends
And try to put things right.

But it wasn't that easy,
Not at first.
In fact, for a while,
Aada's day got worse.

They laughed at her drawings
Of trolls and elves,
Though some felt bad
And ashamed of themselves.

One girl approached, said,
'I'm sorry you feel sad.
I'd be your friend,
But it's just . . . my dad.

He says that pixies
Are full of evil powers.
They make the sky dark,
And like to kill flowers.'

The girl walked away,
And Aada felt lonely.
All she wanted was a human
    friend,
And she thought, 'If only . . .'

She thought having human friends
Would be like being in a bubble
That could keep her away
From playground trouble.

Maybe the pixie was right,
With the words she had spoken late last night.
Perhaps it **was** all the pixie's fault?
With that thought, she stood up
    with a jolt.

Aada said to the girl
Something **REALLY** bad.
She said, 'I'm not friends with the pixie,
That would be mad!'

And the girl stopped,
And turned to say,
'Well, in that case,
Let's go and play.'

And Aada went off
With her human friend,
And felt something new start
And something else end.

Nearby, the Truth Pixie
Heard every word.
And wished she could fly away
Like a lonely bird.

'Aada is better off without me,'
The pixie told her mouse.
'We should go back home
To our little yellow house.'

So the Truth Pixie left Aada
On April the fourth,
Wrote her a letter
And then travelled north.

It took two hundred days,
And was such a hard trek.
When she got to her old home
She felt quite a wreck.

She walked
around town,

Talked to
pixies and elves,
And realised
everyone liked
the truth

Except about
themselves.

On her first week back,
She went to see her brother Cyril.
He was super short,
About the height of a squirrel.

They hadn't spoken for a while,
And Truth Pixie wanted to make amends.
She wanted to know why Cyril
Had three thousand friends.

So she went to his house,
Deep in the trees.
He was having a party
And gave Maarta some cheese.

'Ah,' said Cyril. 'Sister! Sister!
Sister, my dear!
It's SO good to see you
And to have you here!'

'Is it?' she asked.
'Is that really the case?
I feel like these days
I should be hiding my face.'

'Of course, Anoushka.
Of course I want to see you.
In fact, you're so brilliant
I always wanted to BE you.'

'Anoushka?' said the Truth Pixie.
She'd forgotten her own name.
She'd always been 'Truth Pixie',
And great-aunt Julia was to blame.

She'd been the One,
Who'd cast a terrible spell,
And made truth the thing
she now had to tell

But then, at that moment,
Came a whisper in her ear.
It was from an old elf
By the name of Mother Breer.

'Hello, Truth Pixie,'
Said the wise little elf.
'Please be careful,
And watch yourself.'

'Why?' asked the pixie.
'What is the matter?'
'It's Cyril,' said the elf.
'Don't believe his chatter.

Yes, everyone likes him,
But do you know why?
It's because everything he says
Is **a total lie**.

Since the last time you saw him,
He's become quite peculiar,
And the reason for that
is your great-aunt Julia.

She's been fooling around,
She's been rather tricksy,
And now your brother
Is a new kind of pixie!

Like us, now he speaks
Always in rhyme,
But unlike us, he
LIES ALL THE TIME!'

'A Lie Pixie? A Lie Pixie?'
She began to understand,
As her brother came
And took her hand.

'Everyone is amazing!
Everyone is great!'
'Hmmm,' said his sister.
'If you lie, they'll be your mate.'

So she followed him around
As he introduced her to his guests.
More elves than pixies,
Because, he lied, 'Elves are the best!'

'Here's Father Topo,
An elf like no other!
I sometimes wish
He was my brother!'

They went outside,
And Cyril saw a troll.
'So good to see you!'
And his sister said, 'LOL!'

Said the troll:
'I never 'ave been to a party!'
Said the pixie:
'Perhaps because you smell so farty!'

The troll got cross.
The troll began to shake.
The troll stomped off
And made the ground quake.

The Truth Pixie stopped
And felt quite sad.
Was she nasty like Leena?
Was she really as bad?

74

The Truth Pixie ran.
'Troll! I'm sorry! I didn't mean to hurt!
It's just I see truth
And out it must spurt!

But you should know
That I'm stinky too.
Smell my hair,
It stinks of mouse poo.

And as trolls go,
I hear you're quite kind.
You give to charity
And have a curious mind.'

But it was too late.
The troll had gone off in a strop.
'I wish this truth
Would sometimes stop.'

'Oh dear,' said Cyril.
'Truth Pixie, you should lie!'
'I can't,' she sighed.
'No matter how hard I try.'

While her brother made friends,
The Truth Pixie was rude.
'How's your dinner?' asked the chef.
'I don't like your food.'

She offended trolls and elves,
Pixies and a rabbit.
'I'm so sorry,' she'd say.
'The truth is my bad habit!'

The pixie left the party
And went outside.
She said to her mouse,
'I should go home and hide.'

Meanwhile . . .
Further south, far away,
Aada now had lots of friends
With whom she could play.

Everyone liked her now.
You should have seen her!
'You're almost normal!'
Said that girl Leena.

But something felt weird.
Not quite right.
She smiled all day.
But cried all night.

One day, her dad
Peeped his head round her door.
'I miss that pixie.
And I guess you miss her more.'

'Oh, Dad, I know.
That really is true.
It's my fault she's gone.
What should I do?

I've been so silly
And I got it all wrong.
I feel like a singer
Whose got no song.

I think of that pixie,
I wonder what she feels.
I miss her at school
And I miss her at meals.

A friend is special,
A friend keeps you warm,
A friend is the ship
That sails you through a storm.

So I want to say sorry,
I want to make it better.'
'Well,' said her dad.
'Why not write her a letter?'

A week after he said this,
Deep in the Far North,
The Truth Pixie
Was pacing back and forth.

She went to see an old friend
Who was testing a toy.
He was called Father Christmas.
She'd known him as a boy.

'Oh, Father Christmas,
I'm feeling so down.
I lost an old friend
And gained a new frown.'

'You're talking about Aada?
Have I got that right?'
'Yes,' said the pixie,
Staring out at the night.

'I thought she was different,
I thought she was kind.
But really she used me
And it saddens my mind.'

Father Christmas sighed.
He felt bad for his friend.
He saw her sadness
And wanted it to end.

'Listen,' he said.
'Aada did something bad,
But if you really think about it,
You know she feels sad.'

The pixie thought,
The pixie sighed,
The pixie felt her sadness
Was ten miles wide.

'I miss Aada,
I miss her so much,
I wish Aada
Would get in touch.'

Father Christmas smiled.
He could make her feel better!
He went away
And came back with a letter.

Private

'She wrote to me
At the start of May.
She had lots of things
She wanted to say.'

He gave the pixie the letter
For her to have a look.
And the Truth Pixie read it
Like a favourite book.

Dear Father Christmas,

My name is Aada.
I live in Finland. I know
I am meant to write to you
with a wish for Christmas,
but actually I have a
wish for right now. In May.

You see, I have upset
someone I care about. She is the
Truth Pixie.
I think you know her.

And to make it worse,
I didn't upset her with
the truth. I upset
her with a lie.
I told someone that
she wasn't my friend.
But she was the best friend
I ever had. And I miss her.
Please tell her I am sorry.
That is my wish.

Love from
Aada

The Truth Pixie read this
With a tear in her eye.
And Father Christmas said,
'It's okay to cry.

What must happen,
Like ink needs a pen,
Is for you to go back
And make friends again.

She always loved you,
She always had.
She liked it when
You lived with her and her dad.'

So that very night,
Through a sky starry and clear,
The pixie went to Aada
On a flying reindeer.

She landed in her garden
On a warm summer's night.
'Thank you, Blitzen.
Thanks for this flight.'

And in the morning,
Aada looked under her bed
Where, expecting nothing,
She found a friend instead.

'Oh, pixie! Oh, pixie!
I'm so happy you're here!
My life is better
Whenever you're near.

I'm sorry, I'm sorry,
I was such a silly fool.
The way I treated you
When we were both at school.

I thought that being liked
Was all that really mattered.
I wanted human friends,
I wanted to feel flattered.

I was scared of the others,
Felt left out of their games.
But there's something worse
Than being called names.

And that is the feeling
You get deep inside
When you've hurt a friend
Because you have lied

A true friend is rare,
A true friend is the best,
A true friend is needed
Like East ➡
← needs
West

With you by my side,
Everything is right.
You brighten the day
And soften the night.
So, Truth Pixie
What I'm trying to say
Is that I really, really, REALLY
Want you to stay.

99

Yes, pixie, I am sorry.
I want you back here,
But I totally understand
If you don't want to be near.'

The pixie smiled,
And then said what was true.
**'There is nowhere I'm happier
Than right beside you.'**

At school the next day,
Aada stood in the yard,
And did something that
She found quite hard.

As her so-called friends
Laughed all around,
Aada spoke so loud
That her words couldn't be drowned.

'You can laugh all you want
At my old friend here.
You can laugh at her voice
And her pointy ears.

You can pick on me
And call me things,
For being friends with a pixie
And the joy she brings.

She's not like you
And she's not like me,
**But she's something good
That you can't see.'**

'She's not normal!' said Leena.
'And neither are you.
You're friends with a pixie who
Smells of mouse poo!'

Aada smiled.
Aada didn't care,
And nor did the mouse
In her best friend's hair.

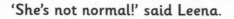

'You say I'm not **normal**.
Well, Leena, it's true.

But why be normal

when you're better

being you?

Normal is boring,
Normal's a yawn.
Why be a blade of grass
On a boring old lawn?

I want to stand out
Like the brightest
          flower.
     I want to
     be different,
Because difference
     is power.'

Aada thought about what she'd been told
All those weeks ago.
She remembered the pixie's words
And spoke them nice and slow.

Don't try and be something
You really are not.
Your one true self
Is the best thing
You've got

The Truth Pixie smiled
And went very red.
It was nice to have a friend
Who said what she said.

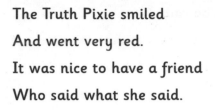

But Aada hadn't finished,
Not quite yet.
'I'm glad,' she said,
'Of this friend I have met.

Yes, she can be rude,
Because she says things that are true,
But that's better than fakeness,
Which comes from some of you.

I want to be friends,
I want us all to get along,
But I'm not ignoring this pixie,
Because that would be wrong.'

The girls and boys heard this,
And some agreed.
In fact, one said,
'Yes, indeed!

A true friend is great –
There is nothing better.
And I like your pixie,
And I'm happy I've met her.'

Of course, there were some
Who didn't feel the same.
But Aada no longer
Tried to play their game.

'The thing with bullies,'
The Truth Pixie told her,
'Is that they'll feel lonely
When they get older.'

'I know this, Truth Pixie,
And I know more too.
I know that things are best
With a friend like you.

When you try not to bother
About what people say,
Those people stop trying
To ruin your day.

If people only like you
For being something you're not,
Then that is a friendship
That's not worth a lot.

It's nice to be popular,
If that makes you smile,
But don't change who you are,
Don't change your own style.'

These were the things
Aada now knew.
Be happy or sad,
But always be you.

You can be quiet or loud,
Rich or poor,
But when you are true,
Life is so much more.

A friend doesn't care
About the size of your house.
And that friend can be human,
Pixie or mouse.

A friend may be a rabbit,
A friend may be an elf,
But a friend is a friend
If they like you for yourself.

And late at night,
From under the bed,
These were the words
That the Truth Pixie said . . .

'There's no point in trying,
To live life as a lie,
It's better to be you,
Till the day that you die.
Be friends with yourself.
Like what you see.
There is only one you,
And that's who to be.'

'I love you, my friend,'
Aada did say.
'Thank you for always
Showing me the way.'

'Well,' said the pixie,
'I should thank you too.
There are no better friends
Than me and you.'

'Yes.' Aada smiled.
'I believe you are right.
And now it is time to say . . .

...GOOD NIGHT'

As well as being a number one bestselling writer for adults, **Matt Haig** has won the Blue Peter Book Award, the Smarties Book Prize and been nominated three times for the Carnegie Medal for his stories for children and young adults. In 2018, *The Truth Pixie* was a *Sunday Times* children's bestseller.

Chris Mould went to art school at the age of sixteen. He has won the Nottingham Children's Book Award and been commended by the Sheffield Children's Book Award. He likes to write and draw the kind of books that he would have liked to have had on his shelf as a boy.

Cover design by Rafaela Romaya
Cover illustration © Chris Mould
Author photograph © Jonny Ring